The curtain first went up on THE MAGIC FLUTE some 175 years ago, in a small Viennese theater. The story, as set by Mozart, was that of a young prince and princess, a bumbling birdman, and their search for happiness in a wonderland peopled by invisible spirits, fabled beasts, the majestic priests of Isis and Osiris, and the imperious Queen of the Night. The prince's flute, whose magic notes had the power to create harmony in nature and in man, protected the hero and heroine on their pilgrimage.

That little Viennese theater still stands, and the sorcery of Prince Tamino's flute continues to cast its spell. When Caldecott winner Beni Montresor undertook a new production of THE MAGIC FLUTE for the New York City Opera, he set out to express the richness, grace and wit of Mozart's music in terms of color and design. The paintings in this volume are based on that production. The text is by the distinguished poet Stephen Spender, who has aimed at a faithful recreation of this eighteenth century fairytale, and who provides new lyrics for Mozart's characters.

THE MAGIC FLUTE

THE MAGIC FLUTE

RETOLD BY
STEPHEN SPENDER
PICTURES BY
BENI MONTRESOR

G. P. PUTNAM'S SONS
NEW YORK

Text © 1966 by Stephen Spender
Illustrations © 1966 by Beni Montresor
All rights reserved
Published simultaneously in the
Dominion of Canada
by Longmans Canada Limited, Toronto
Library of Congress
Catalog Card Number: AC 66-10258
PRINTED IN THE
UNITED STATES OF AMERICA
7 and up

The mountain seemed a dark shield held up against the sky. Over its rim, into the sheltered valley below ran young Prince Tamino. He was pursued by a monstrous serpent with eyes like red-hot coals and a tongue that forked lightning.

"Help me! Help me! Oh, rescue me!" cried Prince Tamino—and fainted.

As if in answer, three Ladies appeared from nowhere and chopped the serpent into little pieces. "Victory!" they cried, looking down at the morsels, now fit only to be made into a scaly stew.

What a lovely youth, the loveliest we've seen.
We must fly at once to tell our royal Queen,

said the First Lady.

"The two of you be gone. I'll stay with him alone," said the Second.

"No! No! You go. I'll stay!" put in the Third.

Then, tired of arguing, all three rushed off to tell their mistress, the mysterious Queen of the Night.

When they were gone, Prince Tamino opened his eyes—to see a strange figure, half man, half bird, carrying on his back a wicker cage fluttering with a thousand wings. Playing on some pipes, the bird-man introduced himself:

As the Bird-catcher I am known
By old and young and everyone.
There's no one with me can compare
For netting birds out of the air.
They fly, bright-colored silly things,
Into my nets on dazzling wings
Enchanted by my merry whistlings.

The Prince immediately stepped forward.
"I'm Prince Tamino."
"Well, my *real* name is Papageno, Bird-Catcher by Royal Command to her Highness the Queen of the Night, with whom I trade these succulent feathered morsels for bread and wine."

Prince Tamino thought: Surely Papageno must have slain the serpent. Politely he thanked him for saving his life.

"Oh that was nothing," lied Papageno. "Just one day in the life of a Bird-Catcher. No need to thank me."

Prince Tamino thought: Surely Papageno must have slain the serpent.

The Three Ladies, returning unseen, overheard these empty boastings. Indignantly they fastened a padlock on Papageno's mouth to stop his fibbing. Then they handed Prince Tamino a locket from the Queen of the Night. Much honored, Tamino pressed the clasp. It sprang open, revealing the miniature portrait of the Queen's daughter, Princess Pamina.

Prince Tamino stared with wonder at the eyes which seemed to look straight into his.

Her features are so beautiful
So speaking, like an oracle
That promises some place
Where living, I shall see her living face.

Delighted, the Three Ladies saw that Tamino had fallen in love with Pamina at sight. They told him now that the Queen of the Night was certain that he had been sent to rescue her daughter from Sarastro, a magician and cruel tyrant.

"Rescue her I will," vowed Tamino, pressing his lips to the portrait.

Then they handed Prince Tamino a locket from the Queen of the Night.

Tamino had scarcely spoken these words than there was a sudden roaring through furious darkness, and the Queen of the Night stood before him. She was dressed in heliotrope—the dark blue of her realms—hung with starry spangles, and on her brow, a jewel cut the shape of a crescent moon. She burst into impassioned speech:

Do not tremble, my dear son.
I see that you are gentle, wise: the one
The fates have sent to me to take my part
Avenging, yes, avenging mine, a mother's ruined heart.
A villain, ah, a demon, wicked, a magician
Sarastro, enemy of all things human,
Stole, stole from me, my daughter, my loved child,
Pamina, by his spells and charms beguiled.
Tamino you have come to bring her back to me again!
When 'neath your stroke the enemy lies slain
Pamina's love, Pamina's love, will then be yours to gain.

The Queen of the Night stood before him.

Having uttered this promise, the Queen vanished, night in night. In her place were the Three Ladies and Papageno, from whose mouth they removed the padlock. The First Lady handed Tamino another present from the Queen of the Night—a Magic Flute, with wonderful powers:

The Magic Flute will be thy guide.
Touch its stops and thou wilt glide
Past fire and ice and precipices
Through ambushes and dark devices
Of malignant enemies.
Its tune will tame the tiger's wrath
Through tangled dangers show a path
And lead thee to thy goal, a grove—
Tamino's and Pamina's love.

The Three Ladies ordered Papageno—who was terrified—to accompany the Prince to Sarastro's castle, to rescue Pamina.

"Don't be afraid, Papageno," they said, handing him some silver bells:

Magic Flute and silver bell
are music that will guard thee well.

"Who will show us the way to the castle?" asked Tamino.

"Three gentle boys will guide you," was the answer. And the Ladies vanished.

The Magic Flute will be thy guide.

Pamina was certainly in need of being rescued, but not from Sarastro. For unknown to Sarastro, an evil slave named Monostatos had fallen in love with the princess and was even now pursuing her through the castle. He hooted, he shrieked; he threatened to kill her if she did not love him.

Just as he really was about to put his hands around her throat, a strange figure appeared at the window. It was Papageno, who had reached the castle and now saw the poor girl prostrate on a sofa, and the black-button eyes of Monostatos staring at him. The sight of the slave terrified the bird-catcher, the bird-catcher terrified the slave.

"Have mercy! Ooh! Aah! Aah! Ooh!" each of them said and turned tail and fled.

But Papageno crept back into the room and said to Pamina: "I know who you are, you're Pamina. There's a dear friend of mine—Prince Tamino —who's head over heels in love with you. Of course I got here ahead of him...."

He went on chattering. All Pamina thought was—"Prince Tamino loves me."

"Why does no one love ME?" cried poor Papageno.

"Someone will some day, I know it!" said the tender-hearted Pamina, loving Tamino, pitying Papageno.

An evil slave named Monostatos had fallen in love with the princess.

Meanwhile, as though guided by some mysterious force, Tamino's wanderings led him to a temple. Across the white marble pediment, he saw written in Greek letters the word ΣΩΦΙΑ, meaning WISDOM.

On the great steps leading up to the fluted columns stood the three boys of whom the three Ladies had spoken. They seemed more like angels, or spirits, than boys. They looked gravely and gently at Tamino and pointed straight ahead.

Follow the path, far as you can.
Be steadfast, silent and have patience.
Thou wert a boy. Now, be a man.
And, among men, oh, be the man who wins!

Tamino bowed his head, then broke out, "But Pamina—tell me whether I shall rescue Pamina!"

At this, the boys gravely repeated:

Be steadfast, silent, and have patience.

They vanished. Tamino was left staring at three bronze temple doors.

They seemed more like angels, or spirits.

Lifting the great knocker of the first door, he struck thrice. Echoes shuddered through the dark within. Then a voice thundered: "STAND BACK!"

Tamino obeyed. He thrust the knocker of the second door. "STAND BACK!" a voice commanded.

Tamino struck the third door, this time with his bare fists. It swung open. He saw the figure of a tall, grave, bearded priest.

"How dare you approach the temple?" The priest demanded. "And why do you come with hatred in your heart?"

"Only hatred for Sarastro," cried Tamino.

"My child," said the priest mildly, "why do you hate Sarastro?"

"Because Pamina is his prisoner. Do you deny it?"

"It is so," the priest said quietly. "But you do not know Sarastro. We do know him. And we are priests of the Temple of Wisdom."

"When, oh when, will I know—and when will they release Pamina?"

The priest looked at the distant hills and his gaze seemed flooded with the liquid blue horizon. He answered gravely and calmly:

When you are led by friendship's hand
Into the shrine to join our holy band.

The priest withdrew into the temple. Tamino prayed:

Oh, darkness, horror, evil night,
When will you be dispelled by light?

Tamino struck the third door, this time with his bare fists. It swung open.

From the green grove beyond the temple, he heard a whispering:

Soon, soon, or never, never.

"Oh, ye invisible ones, does Pamina live?" Tamino asked, and the whispered reply, the wind in the olive trees, murmured:

Pamina lives.

Tamino pressed the Magic Flute to his lips. Immediately, as though he only supplied the breath, and some other being made the music, the air was filled with melodies like light curving upon the air, a sculptured dance. From under the boughs, animals crept forth—lions, tigers, panthers, the unicorn with his single horn of crystal. The music became creation.

And yet...and yet...there was no Pamina.

Tamino despaired.

Suddenly a merry piping interwove the notes of his flute.

Ha! That is Papageno's tune!
Perhaps, perhaps, he's with Pamina!
Perhaps, I will be with her soon....

He raised the flute and wove its melody around Papageno's jagged notes....

The air was filled with divine melodies.

Meanwhile, Pamina and Papageno were being chased by Monostatos and his followers.

Then Papageno remembered his silver bells. He held them on high and shook their rippling tune towards his pursuers.

Still, stay still, the silver sound
Tempts you to a patch of ground
Where you must dance round and round
Tiptoe round around around.

Spellbound, Monostatos and his slaves stopped their howlings and grimacings, and began to pirouette in a circle, as they murmured:

These sounds are so ravishing
So pure and so true,
Every thought banishing
But listening to you,
Dancing dancing in a ring
Then vanishing vanishing.

And they danced away. But no sooner was Monostatos out of earshot of the music than the seven devils which inhabited him all returned. He fell furiously upon Tamino, who had put his Flute down under a tree for a moment, and made him his prisoner.

Pamina and Papageno were being chased by Monostatos and his followers.

A triple burst of trumpets split the sky with gold.

Pamina and Papageno beheld a procession led by a jeweled chariot drawn by six lions, on which Sarastro was seated. His eyes blazed—not with wickedness—but with virtue, love and justice.

"Long live Sarastro! May he live long!" chanted the priests.

"Oh dear oh dear, what story shall we tell him?" shuddered Papageno.

"The truth, and nothing but the truth, though it should destroy us!" cried Pamina.

She ran forward, kneeled submissively before Sarastro, and said:

"Sire, I am guilty. I tried to run away: but I was being pursued by Monostatos. I disobeyed you: but only to obey my mother."

"Rise, dear child," said Sarastro. "I cannot make you love my rule. Besides," he smiled, "I see you love another."

At this point Monostatos ran forward, dragging after him Tamino, his prisoner. But for Pamina and Tamino, all else disappeared. They only saw each other.

It's he!
It's she!
It's true! This is no dream I see.

Pamina and Papageno beheld a procession led by a jewelled chariot.

"Great prince, punish the prisoner!" yelled Monostatos, pointing at Tamino, "and give me my reward."

"Indeed I will," said the wise judge Sarastro. "Your reward is a whipping. And as for Tamino and Pamina, they will be taken to the temple to endure the trials of love."

When they got to the temple, Pamina was separated from Tamino, who was made to share a prison cell with Papageno. Into this place the Three Ladies suddenly appeared. They told Papageno he was condemned to death.

"No, no, say it isn't so," cried Papageno.

"Be quiet, don't listen to their wicked gossip," ordered Tamino.

There was a peal of thunder. Three knights appeared and dragged away the Three Ladies, screaming.

"You have passed the first trial," said a priest to Tamino. "And you, Papageno, will you submit to the trials if we promise to give you a bride?"

"I'd sooner remain a bachelor," said Papageno.

Meanwhile Monostatos found Pamina asleep in a garden. He was about to seize her when a voice called "Back." It was the Queen of the Night.

He was about to seize her when a voice called "Back."

"Where is Tamino?" she asked her daughter.

"In the temple with Sarastro's priests," said Pamina.

"Then we are lost, lost, lost," shrieked the Queen of the Night. She put a dagger in Pamina's hand. "Kill Sarastro."

The fury that so fills my soul
And branches through my veins in fire
Will only be allayed and leave me whole
When my just, ah my most just, desire
For vengeance, vengeance, on the tyrant is fulfilled
And he who robbed me of her, by my child is killed.

With these terrible words, she vanished. Monostatos instantly came out of hiding, seized the dagger from Pamina, and threatened her with it. But Sarastro, wise now to his servant's wickedness, appeared and drove him away. "Do not fear for your mother," he said to Pamina. She will be sent into the endless exile of her own dark heart, the night that is her realm."

Meanwhile the three boys came to Tamino and Papageno. They gave them back the Magic Flute and silver bells, which had been taken from them. Then at a wave of their arms, a table rose from the ground covered with delectable food and wines.

Papageno gobbled and swilled. Tamino only played the Flute.

A table rose from the ground, covered with delectable food and wines.

Just then Pamina came in. Tamino felt her presence run through him like light, but mindful of his vow of silence, he dared not speak. Pamino fled, distraught.

Papageno started thinking again about his wished-for wife.

All Papageno wants of life
Is a girl to be his wife.
Why oh why is no girl here?
When oh when will she appear?

Just then, in hobbled a very old hag, bent double. "I'll be your wife," she croaked to Papageno.

"Are you quite sure you're the only volunteer?" stammered Papageno. She nodded her head. "All right," he sighed, "I suppose I'll have to. Let's get married." At these words the old hag threw away her crook and was transformed into a plump, cheery, feathery, young Papagena. Papageno gasped: "PAPAGENA!" and rushed to seize her in his arms...but she disappeared into thin air. Papageno's ordeals were not quite ended.

Papageno gasped "PAPAGENA!"

Nor was Pamina's ordeal over.

Wild with despair, she seized the dagger her mother had left in her hands, and tried to kill herself:

Oh dagger thou art now my bridegroom,
Through thee, my bridal bed will be my tomb.

The three boys ran in and seized the dagger from her.

"Let me die. Tamino doesn't love me," she cried.

"He does love you, and would himself risk death for your sake," said the boys. "We will lead you to him."

They went to a wild and rocky place where two knights guarded the entrances of two rocky caves. The knights chanted these mysterious words:

Who dares to travel on this dangerous path,
By water, fire, and earth, will be made pure.
Who dares to taste the bitter gall of death
Will to a new and better life endure.
Enlightened by these trials he'll be
Inducted in our temple's holy mystery.

Tamino was led here by two priests. He walked forward without looking back. Just as he was about to enter the first cave, a clear, pure voice called: "Tamino, it is I, Pamina. Let us pass through the caves together."

Two knights guarded the entrances of two rocky caves.

"May I speak to her?" Tamino asked the knights.

"Yes yes, to speak with her is permitted."

"Pamina mine," was all he said, and she: "Tamino thine." And hand in hand, they went along the winding paths to the caves, as to their bridal feast.

When they reached the entrance to the first cave, Pamina said, "Tamino, play your Flute," and she laid her head against his shoulder, letting it remain there as they entered the cave.

Inside, hearing and eyesight seemed hypnotized by the endless crackling and hissing of the flames. Flesh and bones seemed yearning to dissolve, to become the pure emptiness of consuming light for which they were fuel. But Tamino, pressing the Flute to his lips, did not so much play its magic, as let it play him, he the instrument of an instrument.

The Flute played on and as they entered the heart of the flame the furnace seemed to change into the quiet core of a great forest, absorbed in its separateness of a world of scarcely rustling golden leaves. The tune flew on ahead, guiding them as they followed it. It was a cool blue bird leading them back into the world outside.

Hearing and eyesight seemed hypnotized by the endless crackling and hissing of the flames.

When they emerged, the knights saluted them, the priests gave a shout, the trumpets sounded their mighty chord. They entered the cave of water. Here it was so icy that flesh and bone yearned to become the marble of statues. The lovers' heads seemed filled with a whiteness which drove out every other thought. But Tamino kept the flute pressed to his lips, and as it played, the interior of the cave was transformed into the shining corridor of a palace, through which they moved on music-enchanted feet. Almost dancing, they followed the tune which floated on the air above them.

When they emerged from the second cave, behold they saw before them the white marble columns of the Temple of Wisdom, with Sarastro standing on the steps, his arms outstretched to welcome those whose love had overcome great trials. The priests shouted "Victory! Victory!" The great central bronze gates swung wide to let Tamino and Pamina enter in.

The interior of the cave was transformed into the shining corridor of a palace.

Meanwhile, poor Papageno was calling for Papagena, to no avail.

"Useless, useless, all in vain. Well, it serves me right for chattering so much," he mumbled.

He was standing under a tree. Above his head he could see a bough projecting. Feeling around in his bird-catcher's bag, he found an almost too convenient length of rope.

"Well, it must be so," he sighed. "Goodnight, false world, goodnight, farewell." Then Papageno decided to give the world a second chance. Tying one end of the rope around his neck, and the other round the bough, he spoke:

"If anyone—just one person in the whole world—wants Papageno, he will consent to live. Now's your chance. I'll count up to three...."

He stood on the bench and counted very slowly:

"One ... two ... half past two ... a quarter to three ... ten to three ... t ... h ... r ..."

No sound, no protest. Sadly, Papageno took out his pipes to play his swan song:

Goodbye, false world, goodbye, goodbye,
Papageno has to die....

"Well, it must be so," he sighed. "Goodnight, false world, goodnight, farewell."

"NO, PAPAGENO! STOP! STOP! HALT!" The three boys rushed forward and snatched the rope from Papageno's neck.

"Don't be stupid, Papageno. You've forgotten your bells. Just play the silver bells!"

"Bless me," explained Papageno,

What a stupid thing I am,
I'd forgotten all about them.
Little bells with silver sound,
May that girl I lost be found.
Or to put it even plainer,
Silver bells, bring Papagena.

Instantly, Papagena appeared. The Bird-catcher and his bird-wife literally flew into each other's arms.

Papageno
Papagena
How we two love one another
Now at last we are together
Soon-there'll-be-a-little-Papageno
Next-there'll-be-a-little Papagena
Then another little Papageno
Then another little Papagena
Little little
Papapapapapapapageno
Papapapapapapapagena.

In the midst of these rejoicings, suddenly Monostatos and the Queen of the Night appeared and made a final assault on Sarastro's castle. They were quickly disposed of by armored knights. For just as though they were a dream—a nightmare—or dark visions of the night itself—with storm-racked clouds and wandering bats and white wave-winged owls and witches on broomsticks and ghosts in churchyards—they all dissolved in one mighty thunderclap and a streaming down of waters and the light penetrating through a world of darkness vanquished, and the outlines of a happy day coming clear.

Sarastro stood on the temple steps and raised his hands towards the dawn in prayer, and from inside the temple the priests sang their morning hymn of praise.

Wolfgang A. Mozart and The Magic Flute

Wolfgang Amadeus Mozart was born in the town of Salzburg, Austria in 1756. Success and fame came early to the budding composer-performer. Prompted by an ambitious musician father, the gifted boy toured Europe from the time he was six years old, astounding royalty and commoners alike in every capital. Despite a hectic concert schedule, the young Mozart found time to listen to and learn from the music of other men. Soon he was composing equally excellent pieces—sonatas, symphonies, masses, and even operas. Two early operas—La Finta Semplice and Bastien und Bastienne— were written before he had even entered his teens. Triumph followed triumph during those early years. Ironically, the mature Mozart never achieved the public acclaim that had come to him so easily as a child prodigy.

The genius of Mozart became truly manifest in 1786 with the production of The Marriage of Figaro. Following quickly came Don Giovanni and Cosi fan tutte, operas that are wonderfully tragicomic in their presentation of human failings. The Magic Flute (1791) contains the greatest qualities of its predecessors carried to new heights and embodies Mozart's compassion for the Papagenos as well as the Taminos of this world. (At the premiere, Papageno was played and sung by Mozart's librettist, Emanuel Schikaneder.) The Magic Flute was Mozart's last opera; the composer died two months later, at less than thirty-six years of age.

Stephen Spender

Born in England, STEPHEN SPENDER has pursued a distinguished international career as poet, essayist, translator, and co-editor of the monthly magazine, Encounter. He began writing his first poems at the age of 18 and has since published many volumes of poetry, literary studies, autobiographical writings, and commentary on the contemporary scene. Stephen Spender is in addition a frequent contributor to leading journals, the editor of numerous poetry collections, and a well-known interpreter of Continental literature. From 1965-66, he was Poetry Consultant for the U.S. Library of Congress. The present adaptation of THE MAGIC FLUTE, his first book for children, arose out of a deep interest in the works of Mozart.

Beni Montresor

BENI MONTRESOR was born in Verona, Italy. His early books for children include House of Flowers, House of Stars, and The Witches of Venice. In 1965 he was awarded the Caldecott Medal for his illustrations in May I Bring a Friend? A set designer of international repute, Beni Montresor has to his credit an impressive list of major opera and theater productions, including sets for La Gioconda, designed for the gala opening season of the new Metropolitan Opera house. In fall, 1966, he will fulfill a lifelong dream when he makes his debut as stage director-designer in his new production of THE MAGIC FLUTE at the New York City Opera. The illustrations in this book are based on that production. Early in 1966, the artist was knighted by the Italian Government.